AKUNJIERI

EZENWANYI ANNE-MICHAEL
CHIMBUCHI IHUNNA

EZENWANYI ANNE-MICHAEL CHIMBUCHI IHUNNA

"...opaque; rustic; a grotesque account of

pensive ordeal of intense magnitude

contrived in a most compelling suspense..."

Odochi Charity Njoku

Department Of English And Literary Studies

Alvan Ikoku Federal College Of Education

Owerri, Imo State, Nigeria.

"A deft and graphic exposition of some obnoxious but customarily
tolerated practices perpetrated under guise of foster parenting.

A must read for all..."

Community Watchdog Newspaper

"A thrilling narrative of compelling suspense. An insight into the
dark side of unregulated foster parenting. A blistering intellectual
output from a young ebullient scholar. A must read for all literature
lovers."

Hon. Justice Sir Robert Isaac Ewa Odu, KSJI

Retired Honourable Member

Code of Conduct Tribunal

National Headquarters Jabi, Abuja

Federal Republic of Nigeria

TO

BLESSED VIRGIN MARY,

OUR LADY, QUEEN OF THE MOST HOLY ROSARY.

And to all girls and women who are victims

Of any form of violence or abuse.

AKUNJIERI

PRINTED AND BOUND IN NIGERIA
BY:
Edimus & Company, Legal Practitioners, Publishers and Highway
Code Compliance Consults.
1 Aguebube Close, Akiri Amuzi Awaka, Owerri North L.G.A. Imo
State, Nigeria.

ISBN 978-978-49310-2-1

Printed in the Federal Republic of Nigeria under
Edimus & Company ©trademark printing, 2017

ACKNOWLEDGMENT

Fore mostly, I thank God Almighty for the inspiration and wisdom to attempt this writing. The success of this endeavour is entirely His.

Secondly, I wish to appreciate the consistent encouragement I received from my parents, Barr. Chukwuemeka Pius Ihunna and Your Honour, Hon. Barr. Gloria Chinyere Ihunna, LLM, Leuven. The constant prod by my mum really helped to ensure that my dad worked on my manuscript: proof-reading and correcting all errors contained therein. I am highly indebted for such privileged attention.

Thirdly, I wish to commend the total care I received from my then Headmistress Rev. Sr. Cecillia Okafor. I am truly indebted.

Furthermore, I bring to light the present attention and care I have been receiving from my formators, The Sisters of the Handmaids of the Holy Child Jesus especially Rev. Sr. Providentia Igwe (Sr. Principal), Rev. Sr. Anthonia Nwakire , Rev Sr. Rose Udokamma Ukachukwu; and not the least, our very unassuming Rev. Sr. Agatha Abachor. I shall always treasure your stern and firm directives and admonishments.

Moreso, I thank Mr. Mathew Njoku and Mr. Christian Uche Asoluka, my teachers, who constantly challenged me on book writing, mastery of use of English words and for their persistent tease of my intellectual horizon. This book would have remained a mirage without you.

Fourthly, I appreciate my grandparents, Ezinne Grace Adaggu Ihunna (nee Chukwuegu); Chief Sir T.K. Nwachukwu and Lolo Patricia Nwachukwu   for their immeasurable love and prayers. In the same measure, I refuse not to remember my siblings namely Chukwuemeka Aguebube Ezra Ihunna;

Ulummaeze Helen-David Idimmachukwu Ihunna; and Akunjieri Urenna Gabriella Ihunna whose first name I borrowed for the title of this work. I thank you for all the provocative distractions you gave which contributed richly to the creation of this work.

Finally, being a literary work of arts, and conceding that "no one is an ensemble of all knowledge" as my father would always say, I wish to thank the Publishers of OXFORD LEARNER'S DICTIONARY OF ACADEMIC ENGLISH 2014 EDITION.

This tool was not only handy but immensely useful in the making of this work.

This is not forgetting other friends and relatives including my classmates and school mates who offered a word, one way or the other, in order to encourage me. I really do appreciate you all so immensely.

Moreover, I want to appreciate, particularly, Miss Gloria C. Kamalu who painstakingly typed the manuscript of this work and was never tired of making corrections.

Furthermore, it is my humble and respectful excitement to express my gratitude to some of my financial sponsors for the publication of this work. These include Mrs. Josephine Kelechi Iheagwara, Mr. Chris Fialor & Mrs. Olachi Nwachukwu, Dr. Nnaemeka Nwachukwu, Mr & Mrs Chinedu Nwachukwu, Uncle Obinna Innocent Ihunna, Barr. Gavina Chinyereze Ikwuegbu.

I, equally, wish to appreciate Rev. Fr. Collins Ajaegbu, my parish priest, Rev. Fr. Emmanuel C. Nwachukwu, Rev. Fr. Macdonald Uche Nwachukwu (IMAC) and Rev. Fr. Magnus Ebere, SDV, my spiritual director, for the prayers and divine coverage I have enjoyed within the currency of this publication.

I am solely liable and responsible for all errors of omissions and commissions contained in this book.
Truly yours,

Ezenwanyi Anne-Michael Chimbuchi Ihunna

FOREWORD

This book, AKUNJIERI, would properly be appraised within the context of the prevalent trend of the malaise of girl-child violence and abuses.

You will recall that in the developing and under-developed world, reports of hitherto accounts of varied forms of abuses, especially, against the female, have been vague and almost unavailable. Most times, these occur as a result of a combination of both cultural and religious forces which had, for ages, given credence to patriachal authorities in such societies.

In recent history, the trend is undergoing a fast metamorphosis of character adjustments. Education has been key to opening up of furtive and covert practices that had undermined the developments and efficient sustenance of the healthy co-existence and wellbeing of the girl-child.

Many domestic laws and international treaties have recently envisioned and evolved a healthier horizon and hope for the girl-child. These laws covered most crevices of safe-havens for perpetrators of violence against women and girls, in particular.

This book, Akunjieri, specifically underscores the unpredictability of the life of the girl-child and some of the evil of unchecked and unregulated foster parenting. This book, further, exposes the strange terrain that can possibly be exploited by unchallenged behaviours of foster parents.

Albeit fictitious a plot, startling realities derivable from this book, Akunjieri, are actualities today in most homes in the third world countries. I encourage everyone to experience the empathy of Akunjieri's horrific life and the triumphant virtues of her indomitable spirit.

Akunjieri, as a literary work, is further appreciated in the context of the benefits contained within the efforts to overcome the evil of the prevalence of violence against the girl-child and the resultant unrepentant bias encouraged in favour of girl-child education by respective governments, societal authorities, the church and other non-governmental organizations.

Truly, I am overwhelmed by the wonderful efforts by this ebullient, young scholar.

I remain,
Devotedly yours

Hon. Justice Sir Robert Isaac Ewa Odu, KSJI
Retired Honourable Member
Code of Conduct Tribunal
National Headquarters Jabi, Abuja
Federal Republic of Nigeria

PREFACE

Chapter one started with the imagery of the maltreatment of Akunjieri in her foster home. The author tried to access us a glimpse into the life of torture Akunjieri endured. We shall also see in this chapter the reversal of fortune that threw Akunjieri into a life of sorrow and how she became an unfortunate victim of circumstance.

Chapter two exposed to the readers the naked intrigues and conspiracies against Akunjieri by her cousin, Emeka. With the complicity of his friend, Onyekaonwa, Emeka succeeded in framing up Akunjieri as a thief and further aggravated Mrs. Amarachi's abusive disposition towards Akunjieri. Mr. Mbeke also innocently made a false claim against Akunjieri which in turn deplored her state of mind and self respect.

In chapter three, the author showed how Emeka and Adanna mischievously incriminated Akunjieri in an alleged jewelry theft belonging to aunty Amarachi; and the attendant batter of Akunjieri which occasioned serious grievous bodily harm. Even uncle Chigozie's return did not improve Akunjieri's fate. In fact, uncle Chigozie gave impetus to even more daring evil plots to eliminate the innocent young girl, Akunjieri.

Chapter four opened up more dangers to the life of Akunjieri. The plot against her life took a curious diabolic dimension. Charms and other cultic options were unsuccessfully applied against her. Her innocence seems to prevail in her favour.

Nkechi displayed remarkable virtuous traits in defence of Akunjieri. The dark and wicked characters of the rest of the family, in exclusion of Chidinma, were brazenly displayed in this chapter.

In chapter five, uncle Chigozie became increasingly frustrated by the futility of all his efforts to eliminate Akunjieri. Also, a mad man who received kindness from Akunjieri saved her life from impending danger. More heinous attempts were made on her life by the conspirators. Akunjieri suddenly fell ill. The foster family remained adamant in their evil resolutions.

Chapter six contained the account of the outpouring of positive public sentiments in favour of Akunjieri. Her afflictions became well renowned to the point that the second son of the president of the country took a decisive marital interest in Akunjieri. This chapter ultimately show-cased the sweet and loving disposition of Akunjieri as a child well bred and without wiles.

It is instructive to note the use of an Epiverse by the author to express the moral undertones of this work; and further, her efforts to access readers to easy understanding of the words contained in this work by her use of Glossary of Words.

Finally, the author equally used a good measure of some artistic and creative diagrams to illustrate some aspects of the plots in each of the chapters. There is also a deliberate craft on the part of the author to leave a lot to the imagination of the reader as this book is intended to evoke diverse feelings and sentiments. I highly recommend with approval the reading of this book by all and sundry especially students and scholars of literature.

Thanks

Yours sincerely,
Chief Sir Theodore Kabiri Nwachukwu, KSJI
Secretary-General Emeritus
Nigeria Union of Teachers
National Headquarters
Lugbe, FCT Abuja
Federal Republic of Nigeria

CONTENTS

EZENWANYI ANNE-MICHAEL CHIMBUCHI IHUNNA

xiv

EZENWANYI ANNE-MICHAEL CHIMBUCHI IHUNNA

CHAPTER ONE

"Akunjieri, you must wash those cloths fast and make certain that these children are properly bathe; and well scrubbed too". That was Akunjieri's aunt, Mrs. Amarachi, as she shouted from her room. Akunjieri was already at the backyard working on the laundry. She was washing the clothing of her cousins and that of her aunt.

Immediately Akunjieri over-heard her aunt calling, she went straight away to bath her cousins. Each occasion she baths her cousins, she must encounter much difficulties. Whenever Akunjieri wants to remove the clothes of her little cousins, they will start to run up and down naked. Akunjieri would have to chase them. Whenever she catches anyone of them, she will bath that particular one. As soon as she's done with Nkechi and Chidimma, she will fetch water for Adanna and Emeka to take their own bath even though they are her age mates. She will even bring out the clothes that they will be wearing for the day; and when they don't like her choice, they will either beat her or complain against her to their mother, Mrs Amarachi, so that she will beat her as usual.

Akunjieri had finished bathing her cousins; she then went back to the backyard to complete the laundry. Mrs. Amarachi came out from her room and slapped her on the face. "You are always slow in everything you do".

Akunjieri had earlier told her that she had finished bathing her cousins. Nonetheless, she enjoys beating her.

"When you finish washing those clothes, you must mop the floor thoroughly, tidy up the house, water the flowers and plants, cook jollof rice for lunch and then you may take your bath," Mrs. Amarachi screamed at her as she paced out of the house and drove off.

Akunjieri started to sob because of the painful impact of the slap her aunt gave to her. Not long, Adanna and Emeka came out and began to laugh at her. With hateful mimicry, Emeka began to make a jest of Akunjieri, "my maid, my maid, why are you crying? Ordinary slap my mother gave to you and you are already crying. Get used to it. She will be doing it to you more and more every day. So stop being silly. And if you don't complete your work and you dare to enter that bathroom to bath, I will tell my mum and 'she will deal with you even more severely'..."

That was Akunjieri's aunt, Mrs. Amarachi, as she shouted from her room

"Oooh!! Are you still sitting down there? By the time it is fifteen minutes past the hour of twelve and we hadn't taken our lunch, I will beat you myself, stupid girl" Emeka remonstrated and scolded Akunjieri.

"Leave me alone in peace, Emeka. All these chores your

mother gives to me to do, none of you helps me except Nkechi and Chidimma", Akunjieri remarked miserably and mournfully.

Adanna got angry and slapped her, "if you don't like the work Emeka, my mother and I schedule for you, please, you may get out of our house and go to your dead parents' grave and stay there with them and die there, if you want, so that you can live with them in hell"

"All that Adanna said are true" Emeka retorted."You are really an idiot. Your parents are in hell. So you better prepare to join them; pack your things and get ready to go to hell so that everyone will forget about you and your lineage".

Akunjieri could not tolerate the abuse any further: so, involuntarily, she attacked Adanna and Emeka at the same moment without really giving thoughts to it's obvious dangerous implication and apparent impropriety. So, the three of them started to fight. But Akunjieri was at the receiving end because the duo of Emeka and Adanna were stronger than her.

As they were still beating Akunjieri, Nkechi rushed in and struggled the best she could to rescue Akunjieri from their grip. And afterwards, she administered first-Aid on her as she continued to writhe in pains.

Akunjieri sustained many bruises and serious wounds from the fight. Nkechi was so disheartened that Akunjieri was badly wounded during that short-lived fight and that she couldn't do much more than separate the fighters.

Akunjieri was nine years when she lost her parents. Her father, Mr. Edward Nwabueze, was a Chartered Accountant with the Ajegunle branch of Lusa International Bank Plc located in Lagos State, Nigeria. Her mother, Mrs. Otuomasiri Nwabueze, was a Senior Staff Nurse at the University of Lagos Teaching

Hospital. And they were both prosperous as well as very wealthy.

Some envious colleagues in their separate work-places disliked them much. As a result of the high level of their official and social attainments, these disgruntled fellows in their respective offices planned, though in isolation, on how to eliminate them.

One fateful Saturday night, hired assassins, masquerading as Armed Robbers, attacked Akunjieri's parents at home. Mr. Edward Nwabueze, Akunjieri's father, made strong efforts to protect his wife and his only child and daughter; but he was unsuccessful and very unfortunate. He was shot by the "robbers" and he died instantly.

At the sight of the horrifying death metted out to Mr Edward Nwabueze, Akunjieri and her mother, Mrs Otuomasiri Nwabueze, panicked and raced out of the house.

As the "armed robbers" pursued after them, Mrs. Otuomasiri mistakenly kicked one of her feet on a stone and fell to the ground. She let out a loud yell and began to writhe in pains. Akunjieri tried to help her to get up but Mrs. Otuomasiri was overwhelmed by the pains on her legs and dissuaded Akunjieri from making any further efforts to help her. She rather pleaded with her to continue to run until she gets to safety. When they arrived where Mrs. Otuomasiri fell, the "Robbers" did not show any pity despite Mrs. Otuomasiri's pleadings. They shot Akunjieri's mother and began a frantic search for Akunjieri.

Akunjieri hid herself inside an abandoned car. Even when one of the robbers came near to that car where Akunjieri was hiding, and looked inside the car, he couldn't see her. So the robbers gave up the search for her and quickly escaped without being caught.

At daybreak, Akunjieri escaped to Obilande, a nearby village where her grandparents live. Her grandmother, Ezinne Nwabueze, consumed by grief, summoned Mr. Chigozie and Mrs. Amarachi, his wife, to Obilande to come and take over the up-keep and training of Akunjieri, and to move her over to their home.

The whole family was in mourning because two of the most beloved members of their extended family have been brutally murdered. All the same, the family remained not only consoled that Akunjieri survived but also equally resolute in their decision to secure the welfare of Akunjieri.

Akunjieri hid herself inside an abandoned car

When Akunjieri came to her uncle's house, her cousins received her with much happiness and excitement. However, in the days that followed her arrival, they noticed that she was always gloomy. They asked her if she was sick and she answered in the negative. They decided to enquire from their mother, Mrs. Amarachi, the reason for Akunjieri's habit of withdrawing into herself; and particularly, her gloomy countenance. When they heard about the tragic events that happened, they became so sad at the news of the death of their uncle and aunt. More so, her cousins accorded her so much respect because of the poise and ease with which she commands English diction.

Weeks later, after the arrival of Akunjieri, Mrs. Amarachi did not allow Akunjieri to play with her children for no justifiable reasons. She would often occupy her with work. Most times, Nkechi would come to her mother to ask for permission to play with Akunjieri but her mother will always decline her request by trickery saying, "she will soon join you; go on with your games".

"Every time you assure us that she will soon join us, she never comes to play with us", Nkechi queried
"Don't worry, my dear. She's almost done with her work," her mother will always answer.

"But mummy, Adanna and Emeka are Akunjieri's age mates. You hardly give them any household tasks to do in the house. Is it because Akunjieri is not your child?"

When Akunjieri heard this, tears flooded her eyes and trickled down her cheeks. Mrs. Amarachi became uncomfortable with Nkechi's persistent and incisive questions. She yelled abusively at Nkechi in order to stop her from asking any further questions and to weaken her boldness. Nkechi, at this point, ran away from her mother so as to avoid any eventual punishment.

Adanna and Emeka observed the way their mother was maltreating Akunjieri and concluded between each other that

Akunjieri was not really their cousin as their father had told them but, most likely, their house maid. Based on the above misconception, both of them, equally, began to maltreat Akunjieri.

Adanna told her mother that she does not want Akunjieri to be sleeping with her in the same room. Mrs Amarachi did not hesitate to instruct Akunjieri to move her belongings into the store where she will henceforth be sleeping. This arrangement was viewed by Akunjieri as not only agonizing but as well very inhuman. She began to view her place within the house as more of a slave than a relative. What grieved her most was that the bed they prevented her from sleeping on was the one her own father bought for her. Uncle Chigozie carried it to Kuta when their properties were being brought back from Lagos.

Thoughts about her dead parents began to flood her mind. Tears flooded her eyes as she reminisced that she will never see them again in this life. All these thoughts besieged her mind in the face of the harsh treatment she was experiencing from the one and only family she survived to know and live with.

She began to pack her belongings. She trifled with the idea of running away from the wicked attitude of her now 'foster parents' and cousins. Akunjieri was still packing her things when Nkechi entered the room. Nkechi asked her why she was packing her things but before she could answer she was interrupted by Adanna who did not waste time to speak angrily to Nkechi,

"Stop asking questions. I told mum that I don't want Akunjieri to be sleeping in our room any longer. How can I be sleeping in the same room, on the same bed with a maid? Mummy understood my point and directed her to move to the store".
"What? The store! The home of rats and cockroaches!!!" In utter disbelief, Nkechi queried further, "But Adanna, why are you so wicked to Akunjieri? Have you forgotten the beautiful

clothes and pairs of shoe her father bought for us at Christmas? Have you forgotten the Teddy Bear her father bought particularly for you; and you are still sleeping with it till date?"-unfalteringly, Nkechi scolded with incredible alarm.

She began to pack her belongings.

"Oh, don't you know that she actually had parents?" Nkechi hammered on.

But Adanna, sarcastically and unremorsefully continued, "yes I know she had parents, but with a difference"

"What difference?" Nkechi snapped back at Adanna.

"Her parents are dead," Adanna answered with a sinister grin. "She is both an unfortunate and a wretched orphan". At these Adanna's remarks, Nkechi became petrified. She viewed such unbridled statement by Adanna as both insensate and unconscionable; bereft of any drop of human sympathy or feelings.

LITERARY GADFLY Ch1

1.   Did Emeka and Adanna treat Akunjieri fairly?

2.   Did Adanna and Emeka help Akunjieri in house chores?

3.   What did Adanna and Emeka say about Akunjieri's parents?

4.   How did Akunjieri save herself that tragic Saturday's night?

5.   What was her mother's occupation and what was the name of her office?

6.   What was her father's occupation and what was the name of his office?

7.   Where was Akunjieri's new room located?

8.   Adanna and Emeka usually help out in the   house. Is this true?

9.   The room Akunjieri packed into was the home   of what?

10. When Nkechi reminded Adanna of what Akunjieri's father did for her, did she show remorse?

11. Did Akunjieri really have parents with a difference?

CHAPTER TWO

Akunjieri never enjoyed any air of rest in the house. She was always occupied with house chores from her aunt and cousins. Her uneasiness increased by the day which, oftentimes, makes her to experience bouts of headache.

Meanwhile, Adanna and Emeka regularly conspire together to generate more apprehensive concerns for Akunjieri. They devise more strategies of frustration for Akunjieri especially how to maltreat her even more. They made up untrue stories about Akunjieri which increased the beatings she received from her aunt.

Sometimes, when they are accusing Akunjieri, Nkechi will try to shout aloud in her defense; but her mother will ignore her and will still go ahead to beat Akunjieri.

Aunty Amarachi runs a shop, a big shop within the district where she lives. She made Akunjieri the Sales Girl of her shop. Akunjieri was a little bit happier. At least, she can have a little rest from all the crowded work at home. Awfully, whenever Akunjieri did not make enough profit, her aunt will still beat her under the pretext of stealing her money.

One hot afternoon, while Akunjieri was selling some items to her customers, her cousin, Emeka and his friend, Onyekaonwa, walked past the shop. Emeka whispered into his friend's ear what he intends to do to Akunjieri. He told him to show him his uncle's shop so that he could carry out his sinister plans.

 Emeka then approached the shop and took one thousand naira from Onyekaonwa uncle's shop. Emeka told Onyekaonwa to tell his uncle that Akunjieri sneaked into his shop and stole one thousand naira note and used it to add up to her own profit; so, that way, Akunjieri will be accused of stealing from people to satisfy her insatiable appetite for money. Emeka also arranged that when the crime is uncovered,

Onyekaonwa's uncle should demand for double the amount of money she allegedly took. Emeka contrived this evil plot in order to intensify his mother's anger against Akunjieri. Onyekaonwa, Emeka's companion-in-crime, did all that Emeka instructed him to do and say.

That evening, when Akunjieri had returned from the shop, the trouble started. Mr. Mbeke stormed into aunty Amarachi's house with his nephew, Onyekaonwa. He accused Akunjieri of stealing [from him] from his shop. He said that his nephew told him that Akunjieri stole one thousand naira note from his shop so that she can add it up to her own money. Mr. Mbeke demanded for a refund and a compensation of two thousand naira from aunty Amarachi. Akunjieri tried to defend herself but received a sudden slap from aunt Amarachi which threw her into a state of shock.

Mr. Mbeke stormed into aunty Amarachi's house with her nephew Onyekaonwu

"Mr. Mbeke, I am deeply sorry for this regrettable conduct of my girl. Please, find it in your heart to forgive. I will ensure that this does not repeat itself again. Wasn't it one thousand naira that Akunjieri stole from your shop?" Aunt Amarachi asked in a subdued tone.

"Akunjieri stole one thousand naira quite alright but in addition to that, you will pay a fine of five hundred naira for your sales girl's stealing and another fine of five hundred naira for making me to come to your house". Mr. Mbeke explained.

Aunty Amarachi was so angry but did not want to show it. She then gave Mr. Mbeke the two thousand he demanded so that the matter can be laid to rest. Then he left with his nephew, Onyekaonwa.

Akunjieri knew she was about to experience serious pains once again from her aunt. She saw Adanna and Emeka laughing quietly by the corner. So she knew that either Adanna or Emeka had conspired to set her up.

Aunty Amarachi went into her room and brought out a cane and started to flog Akunjieri. She kept on flogging Akunjieri on her body until the cane broke into pieces. She brought another cane and continued the flogging. Adanna and Emeka equally joined their mother in flogging Akunjieri while Nkechi was weeping bitterly for Akunjieri. When the second cane broke, aunty Amarachi became satisfied. Cane marks were all over Akunjieri's body, and most of the bruises on her skin started to bleed.

As a result of the flogging, Akunjieri suffered serious fever, headache, cold, vomiting, and sore throat. She dared not to enter her aunt's room to inform her of the ailments she was experiencing. Akunjieri could not sleep because of the pains from both the flogging and the ailments she suffered. She throws up vomit whenever she tries to get up; and moaned and groaned when she's on the bed.

Akunjieri thought deeply of her parents; different pictures of she and her parents having fun together came to her mind. She wished her parents were still alive; she wouldn't be suffering in her aunt's house with all the heavy work, stress, and pains. Nkechi was very kind to Akunjieri. Nkechi got some money from her savings and bought drugs for Akunjieri to take and feel better. Akunjieri always feel comfortable near Nkechi so much.

LITERARY GADFLY CH2

1.   Was Nkechi also involved in the maltreatment of Akunjieri?

2.   If Akunjieri did not bring enough profit, what will happen to her?

3.   What was Akunjieri accused of?

4.   Did she really do what she was accused of?

5.   Who is Onyekaonwa?

6.   Did aunty Amarachi stop flogging Akunjieri when the first cane broke and Why?

7.   Name the ailments Akunjieri suffered after the flogging.

8.   Did Akunjieri dare tell aunty Amarachi her condition and Why?

9.   Was Akunjieri really suffering in aunty   Amarachi's house?

EZENWANYI ANNE-MICHAEL CHIMBUCHI IHUNNA

CHAPTER THREE

It was in the month of August when women were getting ready for the Annual August Meeting and Mrs Amarachi was also getting ready for the August meeting as well. August meeting is the annual conference of women from a particular community which is attended compulsorily by all women within such community. They converge to deliberate on challenges facing their respective communities and to give assistance to the men on community development.

Aunty Amarachi just finished dressing up and jacked up her handbag. When she had gone out of the room, she remembered that she did not put on any Jewelry before stepping out. So she rushed back into her room and paced straight to the cupboard to take out her jewelry box but it was not there. She searched the second cupboard; it wasn't there. She checked the third cupboard but it wasn't there either. She became very worried. She never goes to any occasion without wearing some gold jewelry. She searched the whole of her bag collections and checked her wardrobe to no avail. She called her children and asked them where her jewelry box was, but they all feigned ignorance of its whereabouts.

Mrs. Amarachi became irritated because her children usually stay in her room to play games, and as a result, very often, they disarray her things.

Adanna and Emeka had grins on their faces. They were the ones who took their mother's jewelry box and hid it. They knew that their mother loved that Jewelry box more than anything she had in her life.

"Mummy, I think Akunjieri took your jewelry box and hid it from you. She often wears some of your jewelry when you're not around and even takes some when she goes to the shop just to impress her customers. And I think this is called stealing. She is stealing from you every time. Mummy, I think you should do something about this; and you are already running late for your meeting", Emeka quipped mischievously. Mrs. Amarachi couldn't believe that the blood of stealing could possibly be running in Akunjieri's veins. Nkechi knew that Akunjieri cannot do such a thing. Akunjieri had never entered her aunty's room before. She doesn't even know the colour on the wall of her room.

She called her children and asked where her jewelry box was...

Mrs. Amarachi sent for Akunjieri. Adanna and Emeka told their mother to let them go to Akunjieri's room to look for the jewelry box there. Mrs. Amarachi was already fuming at the thought of Akunjieri's disrespect for something she treasures so much. She ordered the duo of Emeka and Adanna to search the store where Akunjieri sleeps.

But instead of going straight to Akunjieri's room, they went to where they hid the Jewelry box, collected it and slipped it inside Akunjieri's travelling bag and brought it to their mother. Their mother opened the bag and brought out her jewelry box. Mrs. Amarachi was so enraged with Akunjieri that she took a pestle and hit her on the head and she fainted.

Nkechi panicked and dragged Akunjieri to the kitchen and poured several scoops of water on her before she was revived. After recovering consciousness,   Akunjieri began to experience constant, serious bouts of headache and she hid it from her aunt all the time.

Some weeks passed, Akunjieri's uncle, uncle Chigozie, came back to the house from his trip.   Everyone welcomed him happily, especially Akunjieri. She thought that this will be the chance for her sufferings to come to an end. But on the contrary, more horrors came her way. Mrs. Amarachi narrated all that she had observed in Akunjieri and her behavior. Mrs. Amarachi suggested that they should earnestly get rid of Akunjieri, once and for all. Mr. Chigozie was rather of the opinion that they should not kill her. He suggested to the wife that they should create a system that will weaken her. Mr. Chigozie also said that mere increase in her work schedules is not bad enough; that she will usually get used to the work. He suggested further that they must develop a heinous plan that will make life useless and hopeless for her.

On hearing this from their father, Adanna and Emeka became so happy that their intrigues to enlist their father to join them to fight Akunjieri were a complete success. Already, Adanna and Emeka had manufactured even more deadly plans for Akunjieri.

One late evening, Akunjieri was returning from the shop. It was almost dark and she was walking on a very lonely road. When she had walked about hundred and thirty-eight meters, she saw some men sitting on concrete blocks by the roadside smoking weeds and cigarettes. When she spotted them more clearly as she edged closer, she walked on courageously. One of the men called out her name very loudly but she ignored him. Then all of them came closer in a bid to frighten her anyhow. But Akunjieri was a very clever girl. She dropped the tray she was carrying and squatted down. The men became confused when she began to make animal noises. She began to blink her eyes erratically in order to frighten them. Because it was already night fall, the men became so afraid that they all ran away.

Akunjieri got up immediately and dusted her knees. She calmly took her tray and continued on her journey home. Akunjieri suspected that her uncle's family may have hired those men to inflict harm on her. Akunjieri began to pray fervently for divine protection as she went on her way home. She knew that this scare may just be the beginning of innumerable dangers ahead.

As she was almost home, she heard screams all over the place. The next thing she saw was a huge fire in the bush by the right side of the road. Some patrol vehicles were rushing to the scene blaring their sirens and flashing their lights simultaneously. Many people were running away from that part of the street until the hard, choking smell of the smoke rose very high and spread like a thick blanket, enveloping everywhere. A tanker loaded with gasoline was on fire. A fierce raging inferno. Akunjieri coughed chokingly hard in her efforts to sustain her breathing. She ran towards home as fast as she could.

Mr. Chigozie, Mrs. Amarachi, Adanna and Emeka weren't expecting Akunjieri to come back home that night. They thought that the men they hired had wounded her seriously and she did not have enough energy to come home. By the time it struck thirty minutes past the hour of nine and she was yet to come home, the whole family rejoiced. They thought that Akunjieri was gone for good.

Nkechi started to cry alongside Chidinma over the absence of Akunjieri. They were so upset at the attitude of their parents and big siblings. Mr. Chigozie brought out a bottle of wine to celebrate the eventual successful elimination of Akunjieri.

When the clock struck ten minutes past the hour of ten, Akunjieri came in, all sweaty and tired. Mr. Chigozie, who was watching television with Adanna and Emeka amidst merriment, was not happy to see Akunjieri. Mrs. Amarachi was in the kitchen preparing dinner with her own glass of wine when she saw Akunjieri come in and greeted her. Her mouth opened in astonishment as she dropped her glass of wine to the floor. She was surprised to see Akunjieri in a good state of health in her house.

Mrs. Amarachi raising a pestle to hit Akunjieri

Once Akunjieri had given her aunty her money, had her bath and gone to rest, she remembered Nkechi and Chidinma. She was worried that they might have been crying because of her absence. She went straight to their room and saw them sitting on the bed crying. She did not say a word. She only sat on the bed with them and began to cry because she knew how much they loved her and how much she loved them too. She comforted them and reassured them that nothing bad will ever happen to her. Then the three of them prayed to God asking God to keep them safe from all evil and harm.

Mrs. Amarachi with her own glass of wine, preparing dinner in the kitchen.

Meanwhile, the rest of the family was filled with rage and confusion at her survival. Nonetheless, they had already crafted another diabolic plan to get rid of her.

LITERARY GADFLY CH 3

1. Define the women's August meeting.

2. What particular item was Mrs. Amarachi searching for?

3. Did Adanna and Emeka hide the Jewelry box and why?

4. When Adanna and Emeka went out of their mother's room, what exactly did they do?

5. What did Adanna and Emeka say about Akunjieri and their mother's jewelry box?

6. "Akunjieri had never entered her aunt's room before; she doesn't even know the colour of the wall in her room". How true is this statement?

7. Akunjieri escaped from the men because she was clever. Explain?

8. When Mrs. Amarachi saw Akunjieri pass the kitchen how did she feel?

9. "...the rest of the family was filled with rage..."

CHAPTER FOUR

The next day, Akunjieri went to the shop as usual despite the ordeal of the night before. When Adanna and Emeka noticed that Akunjieri had gone to the shop, they quickly informed their parents. Mr. Chigozie immediately entered Akunjieri's room and brought out her bathroom slippers. They were going to inject a diabolic charm on the slippers. Nkechi usually tells Akunjieri everything she hears or sees within the house. Nkechi never knew about this diabolic arrangement and so she did not worry about anything. It was hidden from her. But she was always watching carefully for any suspicious move. Adanna and Emeka were careful too not to give out any sign of gladness so that Nkechi will not become suspicious and disrupt their plans.

About three hours after Akunjieri had gone to the shop, Mr. Chigozie and Mrs. Amarachi went to a village called Umuobara. In Umuobara, there is a native doctor whose shrine is very deep inside the infamous Forest of Thorns. Mr. Chigozie and Mrs. Amarachi drove all the way to the Native doctor's shrine. When they arrived, they told him their predicament.
"Do you have anything that belongs to Akunjieri?", asked the native doctor.

Mr. Chigozie opened his bag and brought out Akunjieri's bathroom slippers. The native doctor performed some incantations and projected some charms on the slippers. He told them that when Akunjieri wears the slippers, her legs will begin to swell. He told them to come the next day for the final information.

Mr. Chigozie and Mrs. Amarachi went back home and dropped the slippers by the corridor leading to the store where Akunjieri sleeps. They told their children not to wear Akunjieri's slippers. And if any of them disobeys the order, that person will be punished severely.

Nkechi felt that something was wrong. She suspected that her parents had developed another plot against Akunjieri. She made all effort to discover what that plot might be and what next may happen to Akunjieri. All these made her sad. She thought that it might be the end of Akunjieri's existence. And she feared for her life.

Akunjieri came back very early from the shop that afternoon. She was looking for her bathroom slippers. She saw it lying on the floor in the corridor. She took it and wore it. She went into the kitchen to cook and then, she felt a twinge on her leg. She fell down and started to scream. Adanna saw her and passed. Mr. Chigozie saw her and passed. Mrs. Amarachi did the same thing. Nkechi heard Akunjieri's screams and rushed out to know what was going on.

"Akunjieri, why are you on the floor?

What is happening?

And why are you screaming?

Are you alright?"

"Please, Nkechi, help me. I don't know what is happening to me. There are so much pains on my legs. Please, help me". Nkechi became alarmed and dragged her from the kitchen to the room. Nkechi massaged her legs with "Orii", the local Shea Butter.

After thirty minutes of massaging of her legs, Akunjieri's legs felt a little better. She thanked Nkechi for helping her.

The following day, when Akunjieri had again gone to the shop, everyone left the house and went to the strange place, the village of the native doctor known as Umuobara. They went back to visit the native doctor as earlier directed by him. When they met the native doctor, they told him their situation and what they want him to do for them. Nkechi listened intently to what was being said and paid attention to all that was happening .

The man gave them a bag that smells horribly. The bag contained dead lizards and dead fishes. He told them to bury it under Akunjieri's bed that it will give her nightmares which will eventually kill her.
Mr. Chigozie paid the native doctor a large sum of money. They later drove back home. Nkechi became apprehensive and even more determined to warn Akunjieri of the dangers ahead.

When Akunjieri got back, she met Nkechi standing by the door with an unusual appearance. Akunjieri immediately knew that something was amiss. Nkechi took her aside and warned her that when she gets into her room, she should check under her bed and that she will notice that it is cemented.

"They buried some charms under your bed. If you sleep on the bed tonight, you will die," Nkechi revealed.

Akunjieri went to her room and found out that the floor was indeed freshly cemented. She deliberately begged Adanna to share her bed with her that night just to confirm the revelation that she got from Nkechi; and, predictably, Adanna declined. Akunjieri had already resigned her fate totally to God. She knelt down and prayed and went to sleep. During her sleep, Akunjieri had a bad dream. Some men dressed in black were chasing her. They almost caught up with her until she saw a bright light that shone from above and over her head and then she woke up shivering and frightened. It was a horrible nightmare. Akunjieri knelt down and once again, prayed for God's protection.

The next morning, Akunjieri could not go to the shop because Mrs. Amarachi informed her that she will accompany them to a Prayer Center. Akunjieri would have loved to decline going with them but she was given a tight condition that if she refuses to follow them, then she will have to leave their house. Akunjieri had no choice but to follow them.

Nkechi warned Akunjieri that though they were scheduled to attend a church service, they will be going to a shrine and that the native doctor will perform some incantations and he might give her something to eat as part of the rituals.

**Akunjieri met Nkechi standing by the door
with an usual appearance**

"Please, do not eat whatsoever he gives you or you will die" Nkechi warned Akunjieri. Nkechi was so frightful of the outcome of this unpleasant visit.

When they arrived in the forest, they trekked to the area where three bush paths met. They followed the middle path on foot and saw some human bones lying around. When they were almost at the shrine, they saw some lighted candles of different colours. Some of the colours of the candles include blue, white, red, black, green, yellow, purple and gray colours. They passed to the area that went straight into the shrine.

Akunjieri was uncomfortable in that strange place. She became dumbfounded seeing herself in a shrine. She saw wooden and clay images lying on the left part of the shrine. The shrine was covered with red cloths and palm fronts were woven as canopy above the place. The native doctor appeared and smiled at Akunjieri. He sat Akunjieri down on the red stool in the middle of the shrine. He made some incantations and he gave her a piece of kolanut. Akunjieri did as if she was eating the kola nut and then removed it mysteriously from her mouth . Akunjieri saved herself by not eating the kola nut. She was very smart to have deceived everyone into believing that she had eaten the kola nut. The native doctor's gullibility became apparent because the grace of God covered Akunjieri's innocent deceit. No one noticed that she did not eat the kola nut. Not even Nkechi. In delightful mood, uncle Chigozie drove the whole family back home confident that the earlier secret undertaking by the native doctor to ensure Akunjieri's end will become a reality.

LITERARY GADFLY CH 4

1.   What did they use Akunjieri's bathroom   slippers   to do?

2.   Did Nkechi know anything about this?

3.   Why did Emeka and Adanna particular about concealing their plot from Nkechi?

4.   What was the name of the village they entered and what

was inside the forest?

5.   What happened when Akunjieri wore the
slippers?

6.   What would have happened had any of Akunjieri's
cousins worn the slippers?

7.   When Akunjieri went into the kitchen to cook what did
she feel?

8.   What did the native doctor give them that was smelling
horribly?

9.   What did the native doctor instruct them to do with the
objects in the bag?

10.   What did Akunjieri dream about that night?

11.   What did the native doctor give Akunjieri to   eat?

CHAPTER FIVE

Contrary to the native doctor's assurance, after four market days, Akunjieri was still hale and hearty.

It was on a hot Sunday afternoon. Akunjieri was at the backyard washing clothes. Mr. Chigozie, who had become obsessed with anger out of frustration, called Akunjieri from the sitting room. But Akunjieri could not hear him because he was calling her in a very low tone. He was barely audible. He had previously called her three times already until he suddenly shouted her name in a louder, terrifying and callous manner. Then Akunjieri got up immediately and hastened to answer the call. She cleaned her hands on her dress and ran up immediately into the house where Mr. Chigozie was enjoying a nicely cooked bitter leaf soup with a plate of fufu. He was holding a big ball of fufu in his right hand when Akunjieri arrived at the sitting room.

Akunjieri was deeply scared of her uncle and his unpredictable harsh behaviour. Mr. Chigozie swallowed the bitter leaved enmeshed ball of fufu, washed his hands leisurely and gulped down some water. Akunjieri was standing by the door like a statue mumbling her last prayer. She was completely soaked in sweat. She was worried of what will happen because her uncle had already revealed his real self to her; his hatred for her is now undisguised. It knew no bounds.

When Mr. Chigozie had drunk down his water, he leaned backward on the couch to relax. He belched twice before he called Akunjieri's name again. Akunjieri answered him with a terrified voice. The silence within the suspense created by Mr. Chigozie's reluctance to speak became deafening. She began to say her last prayers again by mumbling and muttering some incoherent words terrifyingly. Akunjieri was completely engulfed by horror.

Mr. Chigozie got up and slapped Akunjieri on the face. Akunjieri tried to cry but held back as hard as she could.

"How many times do I have to call you before you answer me? Next time you ever try it, you will not get it lightly with me. I want you to deliver this parcel to uncle Tayo. Make sure you give it to him personally and come back on time or I will lock the gates and doors immediately it is seven O'clock".

Akunjieri at the backyard washing clothes

Akunjieri collected the parcel and ran out to deliver it. She hurried to deliver it because uncle Tayo's house was quite far from Mr. Chigozie's house and the clock was a few minutes to five in the evening already.

Akunjieri was walking on the road on her way to uncle Tayo's house when she saw a small crowd that gathered around a mad man. Akunjieri squeezed herself through the crowd to know what was happening. When she saw the mad man, she quickly turned away to continue on her errand but the mad man saw her and called her name. Akunjieri turned back but was afraid to answer. The mad man kept on calling her name which made Akunjieri even more terrified. She blamed herself for coming into the crowd. She tried to ignore him by attempting walking away but the crowd did not allow her to pass through. They persuaded her to answer the mad man.

The mad man begged her for a loaf of bread and some butter. Akunjieri was hesitant initially; but after some persuasions, she reluctantly went to a nearby shop and bought the bread and butter. She even added a sachet of pure water. The mad man ate the bread and butter, gulped down the water and cleared his throat to reveal the situation concerning Akunjieri as he is reputed to be gifted with the power of prophecy. Little wonder the presence of the crowd around the mad man.

"Akunjieri, when you get to uncle Tayo's house, you give him the parcel". Akunjieri wondered how the mad man knew her mission. He continued; "when he collects the parcel, he will give you some money, make sure you collect the money with your left hand. When you collect the money, step out of his sight and hearing distance, drop the money on the ground and match it with your right foot; urinate on it and pick it up with your right hand; and the money will be usable. Although you will go through many sufferings, it will not kill you".

The mad man looked up and tears flooded his eyes. Akunjieri was completely lost in confusion. Suddenly the whole sky turned completely dark. The whole road became suddenly deserted. She could not see the mad man or the crowd anymore. She proceeded courageously on her journey with prayers on her lips.

Akunjieri got to uncle Tayo's house and did all that the mad man told her to do. When she was through and ready to go home, she felt a sudden pain in her stomach which made her to fall to the ground. She felt a pang of mysterious sore throat and a sudden cold because it was raining heavily. Akunjieri got up and continued to walk, but her legs began to swell and she fell down again. She decided to lay on the ground until the rain reduced. Akunjieri stayed on the ground and slept off. But after some hours, she woke up and the rainfall had subsided. As Akunjieri tried to get up, a car drove past her and spattered mud on her face. Inside the car was her uncle who was enjoying chicken pie as he was driving pass, delighted that at last, his wicked plans have succeeded. Akunjieri developed high fever. She was shivering on wet mud in a thatched kiosk by the road side. She was thinking about her late parents and she was also wondering why her uncle and aunt want to get rid of her. She equally thought about her future. She barely squeezed through to further her education in the best possible opportunity.

She encouraged herself and stood up but was still groaning from the pain on her swollen legs. Akunjieri fell once again to the ground but managed to crawl all the way back to the house. When finally she arrived home, she knocked and knocked on the gate but there was no response. Drained of all strength, she sat on the ground and slept off.

In the morning, Nkechi came out to see if Akunjieri was at her mother's shop. Because she did not see Akunjieri in the morning so she thought she was at the shop. Nkechi opened the gate and what she saw made her to scream, "Sweet Jesus, have mercy!". She saw Akunjieri lying on the floor with mud all over her body and shivering with high fever. Nkechi's screams forced her family to rush out to the gate. When they saw why she was screaming they pretended as if they cared. Nkechi carried Akunjieri into the house and cleaned her of the muddling.

Despite Akunjieri's debilitating health condition the family did nothing until Nkechi begged her parents to take Akunjieri to the hospital. Akunjieri was taken to a very poor and small hospital with very little modern facility and equipment. The parking lot had pot holes all over and some trees scattered dry leaves all over the place. Inside of the hospital premises was a little dark and dirty, and had wooden windows and a small amount of patient beds. In the ceiling was a hole that passed water from the leaking roof. The nurses seemed well-trained and barely managed to administer their skills within the poor environment. The Resident doctor was also well trained and had valid licence to practice but his hospital was just old and there were no funds to do the necessary repairs.

The name of the hospital is Sector Medical Center. The name of the doctor is Doctor Uju. He is a tall, dark complexioned man with a mustache and a luxurious hairy skin. He examined Akunjieri's eyes and mouth and used his stethoscope to check her heart beat while holding her wrist for the pulse. He touched Akunjieri's neck and put a thermometer under her armpit to record the body temperature. Not long, it started to beep a sound. He removed it and checked the readings and exclaim "oh my!" Akunjieri looked at him and enquired what her temperature was, but he did not reply. He wrote on Akunjieri's file that her temperature was 38.5o. He tapped her legs and Akunjieri let out a scream. He wrote again on the file that Akunjieri had swollen legs. He gave it to the nurse to hold. Then the nurse handed him a clipboard to write out Akunjieri's drugs. He prescribed the drugs that would be administered to improve Akunjieri condition.

**She knocked and knocked at the gate
but there was no response**

Mrs. Amarachi collected the prescription from the nurse and looked at it and laughed. The doctor instantly expressed his displeasure at her lack of feeling and warned them to go to a licensed pharmacy in town to get the drugs. He also cautioned Mrs. Amarachi that Akunjieri should not be exposed to any form of house chores. Mr. Chigozie boiled over with anger and resentment at the thought of spending his money. He hurriedly left the ward, started his car and drove off. He did not collect the prescription or go to any pharmacy; he just drove back home. Nkechi was not happy about what her father did and her mother couldn't do anything about it.

Later that afternoon, when Nkechi's parents had gone out, Nkechi took out her purse and brought out some money she saved up over a period of time and ran to the pharmacy to buy the drugs the doctor prescribed. She ran all the way to a pharmacy within the neighbourhood called "Orange Pharmacy Ltd". In Kuta area, it is a very big pharmacy. The environment was well decorated with flowers and smells good with the perfumed flowers amidst the odour of many drugs. The pharmacy was very big and beautiful. The leather chairs were clean, polished and well arranged. There were also some air-conditioning units and some heater units which kept the place cold or warm. Table fans and ceiling fans were properly installed in the pharmacy. The paint they used on the wall was of orange colour. Nkechi said to herself, "No wonder they called here, 'Orange Pharmacy Ltd'". Nkechi saw some posters concerning health matters on the wall. She saw a cardboard paper posted on the wall that says "Midwives and Nurses are very important".

Nkechi saw a poster on the wall

Nkechi approached the section where they sell the drugs. Many people queued up for their turn and waited patiently because the Pharmacist sells original drugs. She too waited for her turn on the queue. When it was her turn, the dispensary attendant called her attention and packaged all the drugs she requested as prescribed,and also indicated the dosages on the sachets. She then left the pharmacy and hurried home.

Nkechi ran and ran to reach home before her parents will arrive. On getting home, she entered into the house and called Akunjieri. She showed her the drugs and also the dosages as prescribed. Akunjieri thanked Nkechi for her compassion. Nkechi pleaded with Akunjieri not to let Adanna, Emeka, or her parents to see the drugs so as not only to prevent them from losing the drugs but also to avert getting punishment as reward.

LITERARY GADFLY CH 5

1.   Why was Akunjieri unable to hear Mr. Chigozie the first time?

2.   What was Mr. Chigozie enjoying in the sitting room?

3.   Akunjieri was afraid of Mr. Chigozie. True or false?

4.   What did Mr. Chigozie want Akunjieri to deliver?

5.   When Akunjieri was walking on the road who did she see?

6.   Why did the mad man insist on receiving some bread and butter?

7.   What did Nkechi see outside the gate?

8.   Describe the hospital they took Akunjieri for treatment.

9.   What was the name of the pharmacy Nkechi went to purchase the drugs?

56

10. What was written on the card board paper posted on the wall?

CHAPTER SIX

Akunjieri recovered from the fever, thanks to Nkechi who bought her some drugs to take during her period of ailment. Akunjieri usually take long walks on the roads which afforded some people the opportunity to ask her of what she experienced. People who heard from others did not believe what they heard. They decided to inquire from Akunjieri; and when they confirmed the same story, they were filled with disappointment. They encouraged Akunjieri not to give up; that God is in control of the affairs of orphans. Many people in the streets admired Akunjieri very much that they wished Akunjieri was their own child.

Akunjieri on a walk

Akunjieri was a cheerful and lovable person. She was also hardworking. Many people really admired her. The Story about Akunjieri's experience spread all over the surrounding towns.

And when the second son of the President, Bayomi Obisenjo, heard about Akunjieri, he thought deeply in his mind if Akunjieri would be the right choice for a wife. One day he sought Akunjieri out. After series of such visits to Akunjieri, his mind was made up. He started to date Akunjieri. He always observes her closely whenever he pays her a visit.

Adanna became jealous of Akunjieri and envied her all the time. She was jealous that the second son of the President of the country, who is a Harvard Trained Medical Doctor, had fallen in love with Akunjieri and is determined to marry her. He is also very wealthy.

The whole of uncle Chigozie's family were no longer comfortable when they see him in their house. They usually will greet him and go inside. Sometimes they try to discourage him by saying that Akunjieri wasn't around. They also peddle fabricated false stories about Akunjieri which almost scared and drove him away.

But he did not want to ruin his chances of marring a girl that is of high moral standard. He tried to confirm the false stories by inquiring from Akunjieri and finally concluded that Mr. Chigozie and Mrs. Amarachi were only lying against Akunjieri. In fact, he began to drool over Akunjieri. After some time, he proposed to Akunjieri. Akunjieri agreed to his marriage proposal and referred him to her uncle, Mr. Chigozie. The family demanded for an outrageous sum of eight hundred thousand naira which also was inclusive of the dowry. As soon as all pre-marital requirements and negotiations were amicably settled, the President's family went ahead to fulfill all traditional requirements of the marriage.

Bayomi and Akunjieri did their white and traditional wedding ceremonies within two weeks of the satisfaction of all customary requirements. They travelled all the way to the United States of America, Ghana and France for their prolonged honeymoon which lasted for about one year. Akunjieri was able to acquire some education during this period to enable her fine tune her knowledge. She was also able to attend two skill acquisition Higher Diploma Programmes in two colleges in the United States which were most enriching for her new status. After the most thrilling and engaging honeymoon, they, finally, came back to Nigeria.

Akunjieri was very glad she was back to where she belonged. She really missed home.

"Oh My!!! Home is home. Nowhere is better than home."

She has so many people she desire to visit and talk to. But she had her mind more on her cousins. She missed them so much that it kept on disturbing her. Her mind stayed permanently on them throughout her honeymoon but she tried not to allow it to interfere with her excitement, studies and romance.

Until one fateful day, she decided to pay a visit to her cousins. She drove into their compound with her personal Toyota Sequoia SUV. She stepped out of her car alone which was not normal because she is always accompanied by three secret service agents wherever she goes. She knocked on the door and walked in. She noticed that the compound was the same way she left it one year and three months ago. Nobody was at home by that time. So Akunjieri stayed a little longer.

The gate opened and Nkechi stepped into the house. She just came back from the farm.

"Oh my God! Who are you, and what are you doing in my father's house?".

Akunjieri unveiled herself to Nkechi and Nkechi was filled with tears of Joy. She was so happy to see Akunjieri again. Akunjieri and Nkechi had a very long and exciting discussion before she departed. Akunjieri, finally, departed after spending thirty minutes only with Nkechi on a promise to return the visit.

When Nkechi's parents came back, Nkechi told them about Akunjieri's visit and their discussion. Nkechi's parents did not care about anything Nkechi said but Adanna was so furious that Akunjieri had come back and entered into their house. She wished Akunjieri was dead or that she was married to her husband instead. She was completely consumed by jealousy and couldn't hide her resentment.

After a few years, Nkechi, Chidinma and Emeka got married and departed to their respective new homes. Emeka became a carpenter with a small shop and his wife was a petty trader. Chidinma was jobless and her husband was a fish monger. Nkechi was a fish seller and her husband was a butcher. Akunjieri finished her university and got employed as a lecturer in Madonna University, Abuja. She trained Nkechi and Chidinma's children in school. Akunjieri's husband, Bayomi Obisenjo, built a Gas Station for Emeka and a Super Market for his wife.

Akunjieri single-handedly built four Gas Stations. She gave Chidinma and her husband two of the Gas Stations. She also gave Nkechi and her husband the other two Gas Stations. She built a primary school for Emeka's wife and named it, "VICTORY IS SWEET PRIMARY SCHOOL". Akunjieri, very often, sends gifts to Nkechi like money, fruits and food stuffs. She built a restaurant for Chidinma to run. Akunjieri bought two big black Lexus Jeeps for her uncle and Aunt. She also bought a white Jeep for Adanna and filled it with a lot of gift items; but Adanna rejected it. Adanna was still full of melancholy.

Mr. Chigozie and aunt Amarachi regretted the way they had treated Akunjieri in the past and begged for forgiveness.

Akunjieri forgave them. Adanna's parents pleaded with her to beg for forgiveness but she swore that she will never beg for forgiveness from Akunjieri.

Adanna began to feel uncomfortable for not staying married. She was tired of her fellow women mocking her of not getting married. Some even gave her the nick-name, "single mama". She could no longer take the pressure any longer.

One day, she put a white board in front of her gate with the inscription, "unmarried lady available" A handsome young man came and proposed to her and she agreed.

Adanna had gotten married to many men but she is always thrown out of marriage on each occasion. The first man she got married to divorced her because she was always nagging and bed-wetting. The second man that married her threw her out because she wakes up by 10:00am in the morning and before she could get to the market, the women had already finished buying every fresh product in the market. The third man threw her out because she is abusive, unhygienic and, unfortunately, a bad cook. The fourth man she got married to deserted her because she could not bear him any child, and she regularly keeps late night and always drunk.

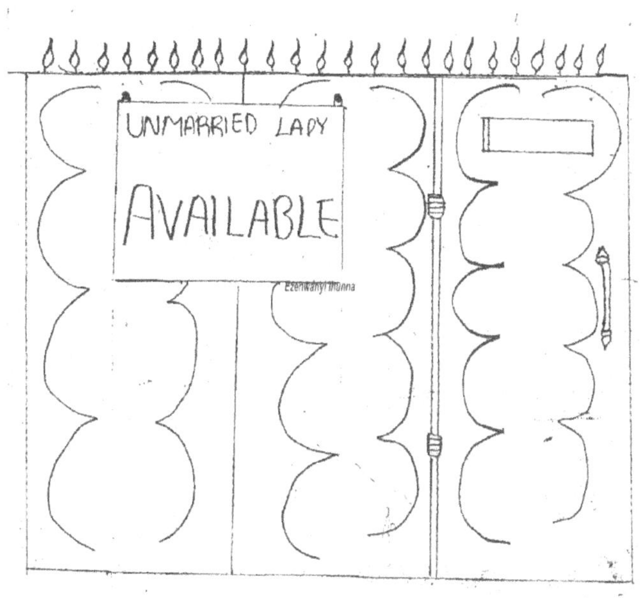

The white board hanging from Adanna's gate

All Adanna's children turned out to be useless in life as a result of her broken homes. Despite all these shortcomings, Adanna became lucky, once again. She got married to her new husband and entered into her new home. But her new husband, Engr. Danladi Garuba, keeps late nights and daily leaves the house around 1:00am or 2:00am in the wee hours of the morning.

One fateful night, Engr. Danladi Garuba without provocation attacked Adanna , his new wife, with a knife in order to wound her. She fought back in self defence and got bruises all over her body. Luckily, Adanna ran out of the house and escaped while he chased after her with the knife.

Adanna managed to escape because she was smart enough to pick up a big, rough and heavy stone from the ground which she threw at him and it landed on his forehead; and neutralized him.

Adanna escaped to her parent's home with blood gushing out all over her body. She was rushed to the hospital for treatment. She remained unconscious for eight hours. When Akunjieri heard of her ordeal, she came to visit her and brought her a bouquet of flowers. She spent time by her bedside praying for her quick recovery before she later left the hospital. When Adanna regained consciousness, she noticed a bouquet of flower on the table. She admired it so much but when she read the little note attached to the flowers by Akunjieri, to everybody's disquiet, she cut the flowers to pieces with scissors in angry rejection of Akunjieri's kind gesture. Adanna remained unremorseful and unrepentant.

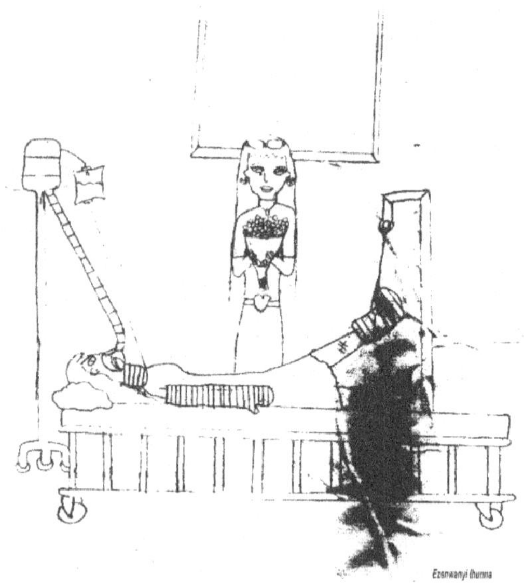

Akunjieri with Bouquet of flowers

Rumours spread everywhere that Adanna got married to a cultist and barely escaped with her life. People in the streets began to advise their children to be of high moral behaviour and disciplined so that they will be useful in life. They must never be as disobedient and heartless, a person, as Adanna.

Akunjieri enjoyed a wonderful, blissful and prosperous marriage with Bayomi Obisenjo; and their union was blessed with four children namely Chidiadi, Uloma, Chiedozie and Nkechi named after the same Nkechi that remained her best confidant.

LITERARY GADFLY CH 6

1.   To who was Akunjieri engaged?

2.   Why was Adanna jealous of Akunjieri?

3.   How much did Uncle Chigozie's family demand   as dowry for Akunjieri?

4.   Why did the family frame fake scary stories   about Akunjieri?

5.   When Akunjieri presented her gifts to her uncle and aunt, what were their reaction?

6.   Why was Adanna taken to the hospital?

7.   What lessons did you learn from this story?

Some pay good for evil;
Some pay evil for good.
Forgiveness and understanding,
Should be common-placed.
Be good in your life,
To achieve success like Akunjieri.

Eschew avarice, avoid envy;
Melancholy debilitates: brews jealousy.
A bumper harvest of nothing good
Ensues from the raging fire of evil.
Victorious were all but Adanna
Lost eternal marriage to unrepentance.

A

Accord	:	harmony, agreement, settlement.
Afford	:	met the expense for, have the funds for, pay for.
Agonizing	:	heartbreaking, unbearable, painful.
Ailment	:	illness, weakness, compliant.
Allegedly	:	supposedly, purportedly.
Amidst	:	surrounded, middle of, encompassed by, amongst.
Amiss	:	wrong, faulty, improper.
Apparent	:	clear, noticeable, plain.
Assassin	:	killer, hired-gun, murderer.
Assurance	:	declaration, promise, guarantee.
Astonishment	:	surprise, bewilderment, amazement.
Attainment	:	achievement, accomplishment, success.
Avert	:	prevent, forestall, ward off.
Awfully	:	appallingly, dreadfully, horribly.

B

Belch   :   to expel gas loudly or rudely from the
stomach   through the   mouth, burp.

Bereft   :   deprived of, lacking, stripped of, robbed
of.
Boldness   :   valor, daring, audacity.
Bout   :   a period of something usually painful or
unpleasant
Bruise   :   discoloration, bash, damage.
Bulge   :   lump, swelling, prominence.

C

Callous   :   heartless, cold-hearted, cruel.
Chartered Accountant: a qualified accountant licensed to
practice.
Chores   :   household tasks, errands, responsibilities.

Clipboard   :   a flat piece of rigid materials, such as card
or plastic with a clip at one end under which papers can be
held.
Colleagues   :   co-workers, work mates.
Conspire   :   to secretly plot or makes plan together in
respect of something bad or illegal.
Contrive   :   plan, scheme, arrange, plot.
Countenance   :   approved of, put up with, expression.

D

Deafening   :   vociferous, boisterous, rowdy.
Debilitating   :   weakening,. incapacitating, devastating.
Delightful   :   pleasant, pleasing, bringing satisfaction,
enjoyment or   pleasure.
Devise   :   think up, work out, develop.

Diabolic	:	showing wickedness, extremely evil or cruel, satanic.
Diction	:	elocution, accent, articulation.
Disarray	:	confusion, dismay, disorder.
Disgruntle	:	dissatisfy, displease, disappoint.
Dishearten	:	cause dejection, sadden, dampen the spirits.
Dissuade	:	deter, persuade against, discourage.
District	:	area, locality, ward.
Drool	:	salivate, dribble, slobber.

E

Ease	:	straightforwardness, effortlessness, no difficulty.
Eliminate	:	purge, remove, get rid of.
Engulf	:	swallow up, overwhelm, overcome.
Enquire	:	to ask, to make an enquiry.
Enraged	:	angered, made furious, made full of rage.
Event	:	an occurrence, an outcome, end result.
Eventual	:	pertaining to events, final, ultimate.
Envious	:	feeling or exhibiting envy, jealously desiring the excellence or good fortune of another, maliciously grudging, spiteful.

F

Fateful	:	significant, critical, crucial.
Feigned	:	pretend, artificial, insincere
Fellow	:	member, associate, colleague.
Fervently	:	enthusiastically, zealously, passionately.

G

Gloomy	:	ominous, dark, depressing.

Grieve : feel sad, lament, be upset.
Grin : smile, beam, smirk.
Grip : hold, grasp, grab, clench, clutch, seize.
Gullibility : lack of caution, trustfulness, innocence.

H

Habit : routine, practice, pattern.
Hale and hearty : sound, robust, energetic.
Intolerable : insupportable, unbearable, unendurable.
Hesitant : timid, doubtful, undecided.
Hesitate : shilly-shally, waver, falter.
Hire : take into service, engage, employ.
Horrifying : terrible, appalling, gruesome.

I

Idiot : a common term for a person of low general intelligence, an adult with low mental capacity.
Ignorance : lack of knowledge, unawareness, blindness.
Impact : collision, shock, contact.
Impropriety : indecency, lack of decorum, bad taste.
Incisive : perceptive, penetrating, sharp.
Infest : plague, overrun, riddle.
Inhuman : coldblooded, ruthless, brutal.
Innumerable : countless, immeasurable, infinite.
Insensate : lacking feeling, numbed, insensitive.
Involuntary : spontaneous, instinctive, unthinking,
Irritated : aggravated, goaded, annoyed.
Isolated : inaccessible, cut-off, secluded.

J

Jest : tease, prank, banter.

Justifiable	:	permissible, reasonable, valid.

K

L

Laundry	:	a washing, a place or room where laundry is done.
Leaned back	:	recline, tilt, slant.
Lineage	:	ancestry, extraction, family tree, heredity.
Loud	:	thunderous, earsplitting, noisy.

M

Maltreat	:	hurt, injure, abuse.
Masquerading	:	masked, camouflaged, concealed.
Merriment	:	cheerfulness, fun, laughter.
Meted-out	:	unleash on, treat.
Mimicry	:	parody, impersonation, imitation.
Mischievously	:	roguishly, impishly, naughtily.
Misconception	:	mistaken belief, misconstruction, misunderstanding.
Miserable	:	depressed, dejected, despondent.
Mop	:	wash, wipe, cleanup.
Mournfully	:	dolefully, desolately, sorrowfully.
Muddle	:	mix-up, mess, tangle.
Mumbling	:	tongue-tied, inarticulate, incoherent.
Murder	:	kill, assassinate, put to death.
Mutter	:	murmur, grumble, mumble.

N

Negative	:	unenthusiastic, unhelpful, depressing.
No avail	:	no benefit, no reward, no advantage.
Nonetheless	:	on the other hand, even so, however.

O

Obsessed	:	gripped, passionate, preoccupied.
Often times	:	frequently, repeatedly.
Ordeal	:	tribulation, torments, trial.
Overheard	:	to hear something that wasn't meant for one's ears.
Overwhelmed	:	over power emotionally, engulf, surge-over, crush.

P

Pace	:	speed, swiftness, tempo.
Panic	:	dread, fright, horror.
Peddle	:	advertise, publicize, advocate.
Persistent	:	relentless, pushy, continual.
Pestle	:	crusher, pounder, rod.
Petrified	:	scared stiff, frightened, alarmed.
Poise	:	good posture, carriage, dignity.
Prescription	:	recommendation, treatment, remedy, instruction.
Previously	:	earlier, before-hand, formerly.
Prosperous	:	affluent, well-off, successful.

Q

Query	:	inquiry, question mark, or question.
Quip	:	clever remark, jibe, retort.

R

Race	:	chase, pursuit, event, compete.
Reminisce	:	muse over, recollect, bring to mind.
Remonstrate	:	dispute, squabble, oppose.

Resentment   :   anger, bitterness, hatred.
Resolute   :   firm, staunch, determine.
Respective   :   personal, particular, relevant.
Revived   :   re-energized, rejuvenated, re
invigorated.

S

Sarcastically   :   derisively, ironically,   mockingly.
Schedule   :   agenda, time-table, programme.
Scold   :   reprimand, rebuke, admonish.
Simultaneously: at the same time, all together, at once.
Sinister   :   creepy, ominous, evil.
Sob   :   weep, snivel, moan.
Squat   :   sit on your heels, cower, bend.

T

Tolerate   :   bear, put up with, endure.
Tragic   :   disastrous, catastrophic, awful.
Trek   :   walk, march, trudge.
Trickle   :   seep, drip, filter.
Trifle   :   touch, bit, drop.
Twinge   :   ache, cramp, spasm.

U

Unconscionable   :   fleeting consideration,
thoughtlessness, disregard.
Undisguised   :   open, obvious, evident.
Uneasiness   :   apprehension, disquiet, agitation.
Unfortunate   :   ill-fated, adverse, regrettable.
Unremorsefully   :   impenitently, unashamedly,
unapologetically.

V

W

Wealthy	:	well-off, affluent, prosperous.
Well-scrubbed	:	thoroughly washed
Whereabouts	:	location, situation, position.
Withdraw	:	remove, take out, pull out, leave.
Work-place	:	place of work, office, headquarters.

Writhe	:	squirm, wriggle, struggle, twist.

X

Y

Yell	:	scream, shriek, howl, bellow.

Z

75

ABOUT THE AUTHOR

Akunjieri is a literary construction which attempts to portray an allegory of violence and repressive realities which confront the girl-child in most economies of the third world countries. Akunjieri, bedeviled by misfortune of loss of her parents at tender age, became assailed by torrents of unpredictable and persistent barrage of wickedness. Being born of the roots of honesty and nobility, her intrinsic virtuous resourcefulness was tried, without doubt, to the extremes. Her triumph lends a loud credence to the very nature that begot her. Through perseverance, she overcame her fears, doubts and troubles; and, ultimately, assumed the height of crowning glory over all her assailants. Even so, this book underpins the need for more, thorough and robust regulations in respect of the administrations of foster homes and, more particularly, the protection, welfare and education of the girl-child in a world of increasing patriachal leanings prejudiced by hypocritical approach to justice delivery.

Ezenwanyi Anne-Michael Chimbuchi Ihunna was born on 15th March, 2005 at Universitaire Ziekenhuizen Gathsiusberg, Leuven, Belgium to Barr. Chukwuemeka Pius Ihunna and Hon. Barr. Gloria Chinyere Ihunna under the clinical supervision of Prof. Dr. M. Hanssens. Ezenwanyi, in 2006, started her education at HHCJ St. Aloysius Int'l Nursery/Primary School Area 3, Garki Abuja. In 2010, her studies continued in HHCJ Assumpta Nursery/Primary School Owerri, Imo State. Ezenwanyi is currently at HHCJ Assumpta Girls' Model Secondary School, Area G, New Owerri, Imo State. AKUNJIERI is her first published novel and shall precede the immediate publications of her two other books: THE BRIGHTEST FUTURE and POT BEFORE MARRIAGE.

www.ingramcontent.com/pod-product-compliance
Lightning Source LLC
Chambersburg PA
CBHW051347150726
48000CB00003B/1080